SLEEPY
BEAR

Lydia Dabcovich

SLEEPY BEAR

PUFFIN BOOKS

for Emilie McLeod
who understands bears

Unicorn is a registered trademark of Dutton Children's Books.

Library of Congress number 81-9729
ISBN 0-14-054785-1

Published in the United States by Dutton Children's Books,
a division of Penguin Books USA Inc.
375 Hudson Street, New York, N.Y. 10014
Editor: Emilie McLeod   Designer: Riki Levinson

Printed in Hong Kong by South China Printing Co.
First Unicorn Edition 1985
15   16   17   18   19   20

IT'S GETTING COLD.

LEAVES ARE FALLING.

BIRDS ARE LEAVING

AND BEAR IS SLEEPY.

HE FINDS A CAVE.

AND SNOWS.

BUT BEAR IS COZY
IN HIS CAVE.

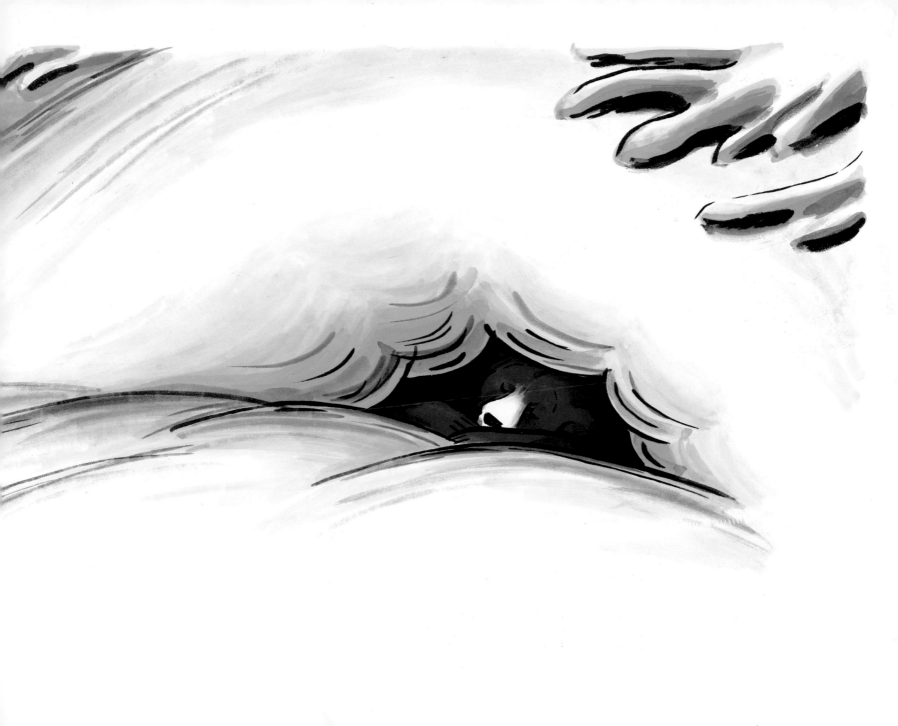

THE SUN COMES OUT AGAIN.

BIRDS COME BACK.

BUGS COME BACK.

BEES COME BACK.

BEAR REMEMBERS HONEY.
HE FOLLOWS THE BEES.